ISBN-13: 978-1-338-20923-5
ISBN-10: 1-338-20923-X

1 2 3 4 5 6 7 8 9 10   40   26 25 24 23 22 21 20 19 18 17

CONTENTS

THE RED TREE

shaun tan

sometimes the day begins
with nothing to look forward to

and things go from bad to worse

darkness

overcomes you

nobody understands

the world is a

deaf machine

472

473

sometimes you wait

and wait

and wait

and wait

and wait

and wait

and wait

but nothing ever happens

then all your troubles come at once

wonderful things
are
passing
you
by

terrible fates are
inevitable

sometimes
you just don't know
what you are
supposed to
do

or

who

you   meant
    are

       to

       be

or

where
you are

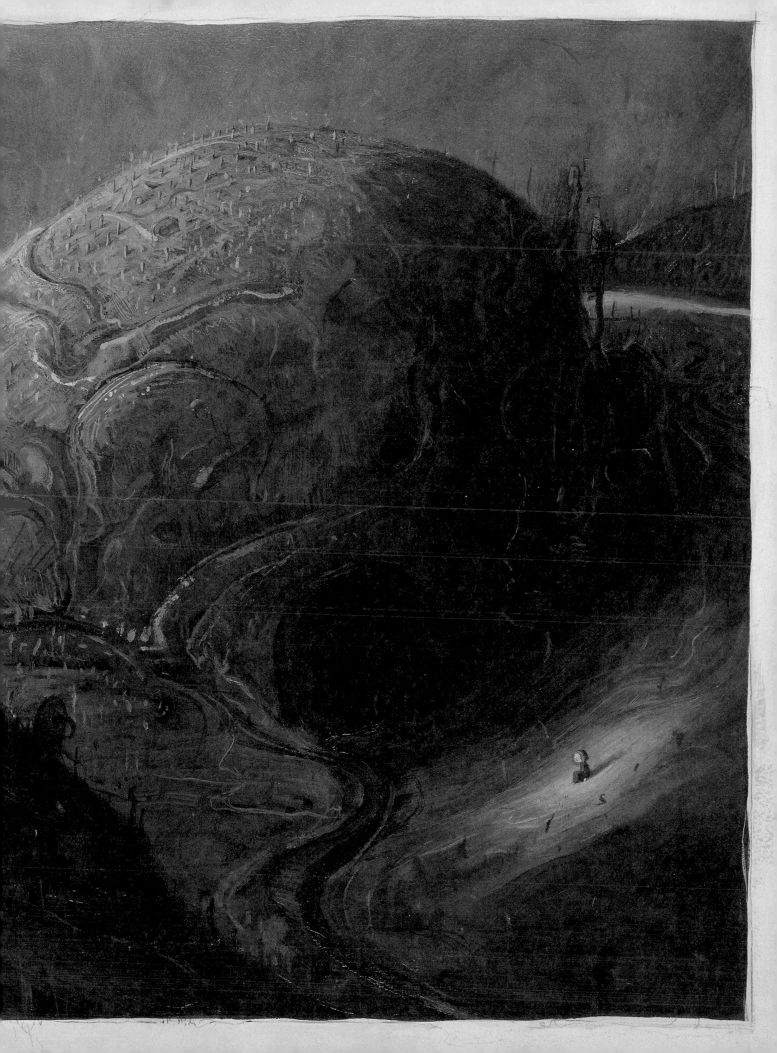

and the day seems to end
the way it began

but suddenly there it is
right in front of you

bright and vivid

quietly waiting

just as you imagined it would be

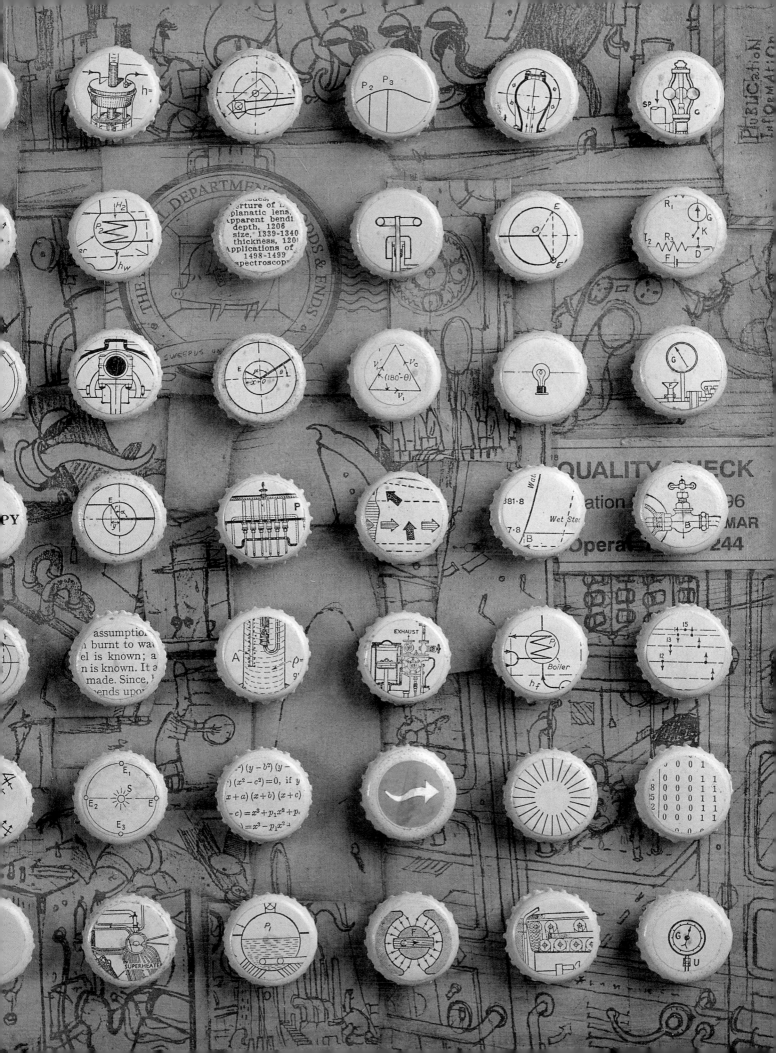

The LoST THiNG

by Shaun Tan.

A tale for those who have more important things to pay attention to

40d.

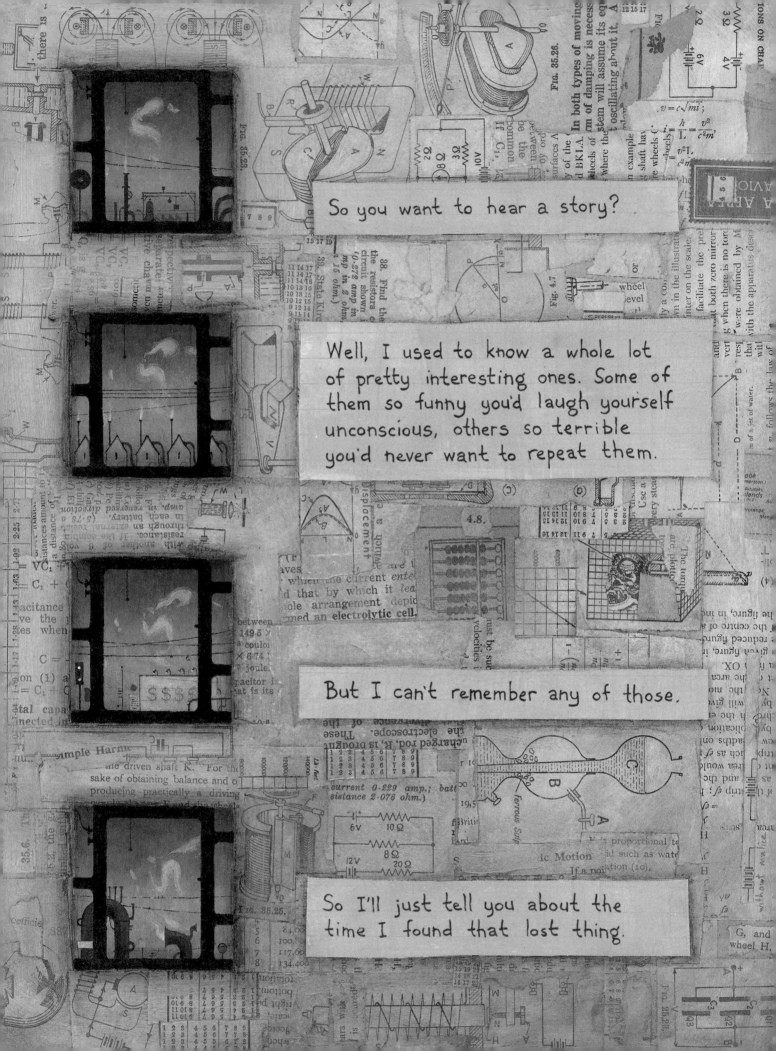

So you want to hear a story?

Well, I used to know a whole lot of pretty interesting ones. Some of them so funny you'd laugh yourself unconscious, others so terrible you'd never want to repeat them.

But I can't remember any of those.

So I'll just tell you about the time I found that lost thing.

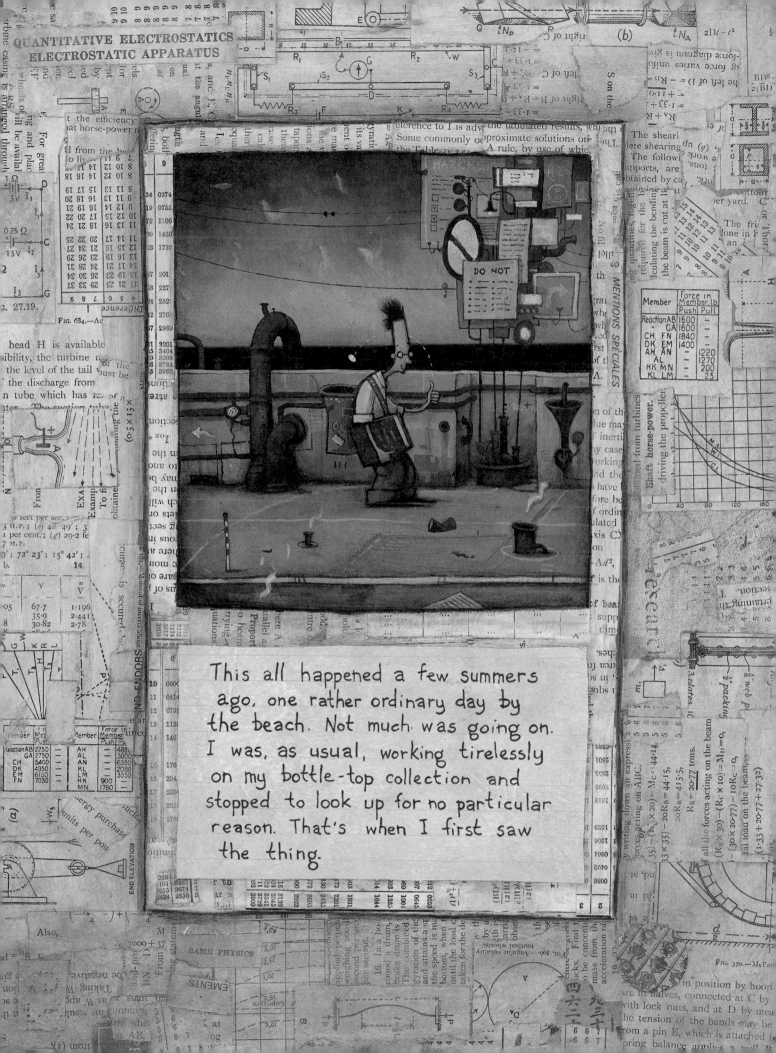

This all happened a few summers ago, one rather ordinary day by the beach. Not much was going on. I was, as usual, working tirelessly on my bottle-top collection and stopped to look up for no particular reason. That's when I first saw the thing.

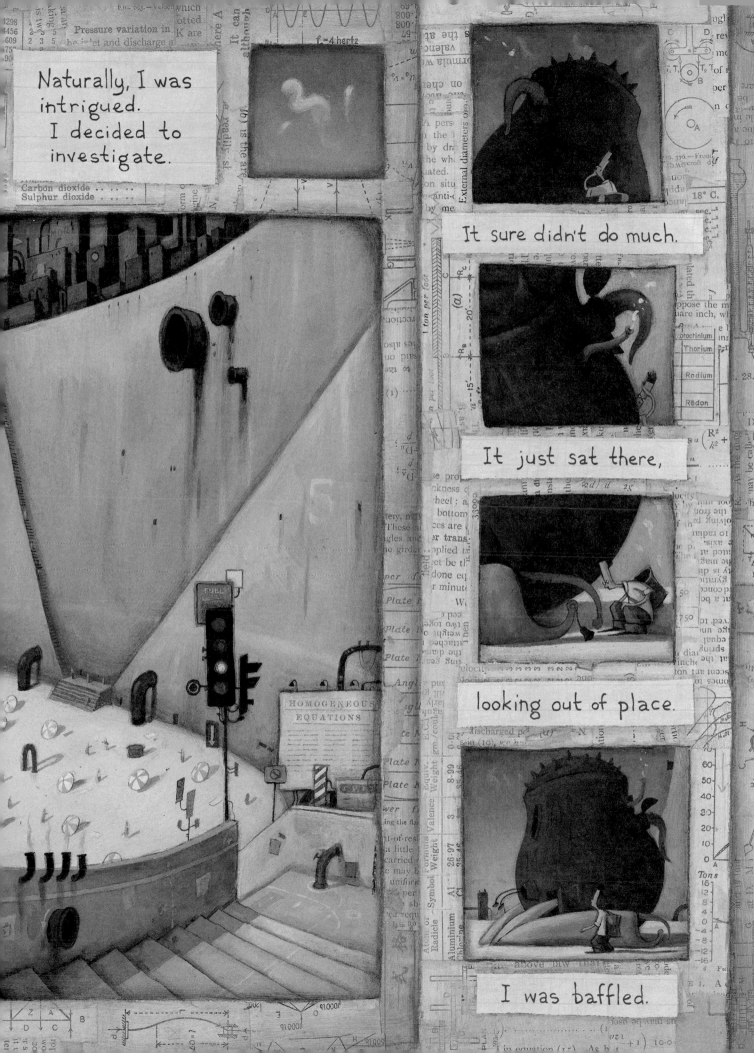

It was quite friendly though, once I started talking to it.

ANTI-LOGARITHMS

I played with the thing for most of the afternoon. It was great fun, yet I couldn't help feeling that something wasn't quite right.

Exercise 7b*

As the hours slouched by, it seemed less and less likely that anybody was coming to take the thing home. There was no denying the unhappy truth of the situation. It was <u>lost</u>.

I asked a few people if they knew anything about it, but nobody was very helpful.

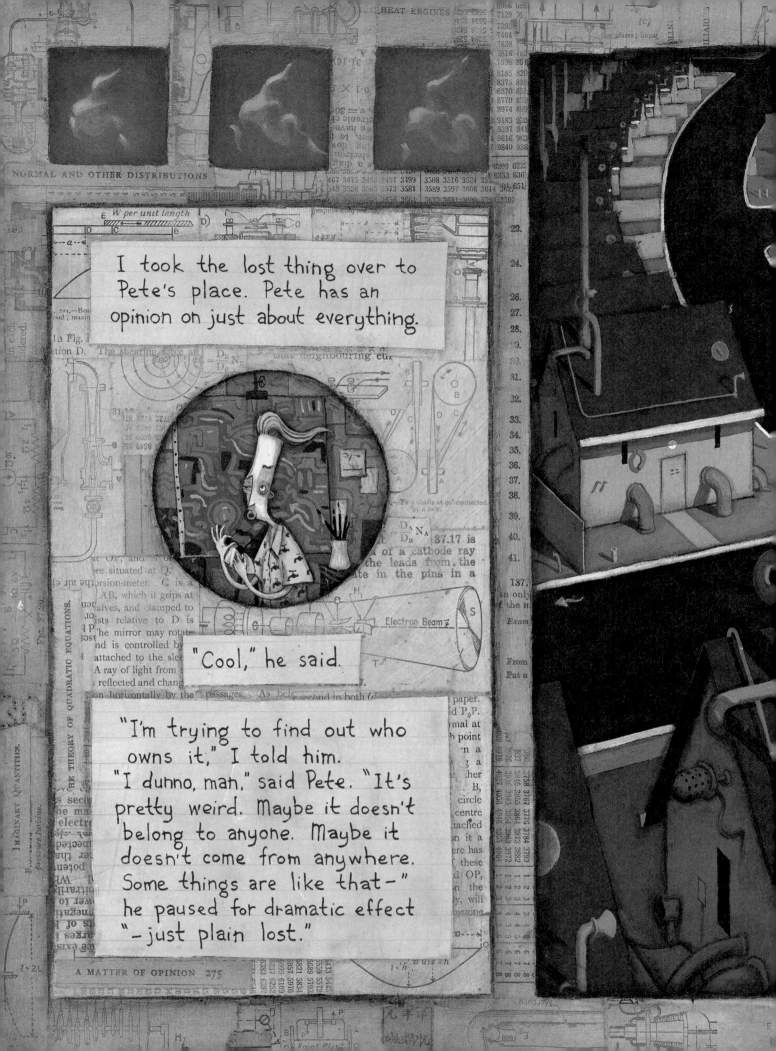

I took the lost thing over to Pete's place. Pete has an opinion on just about everything.

"Cool," he said.

"I'm trying to find out who owns it," I told him.
"I dunno, man," said Pete. "It's pretty weird. Maybe it doesn't belong to anyone. Maybe it doesn't come from anywhere. Some things are like that–" he paused for dramatic effect "–just plain lost."

There was nothing left to do but take the thing home with me. I mean, I couldn't just leave it wandering the streets. Plus I felt kind of sorry for it.

My parents didn't really notice it at first.
Too busy discussing current events, I guess.

Eventually I had to point it out to them.
"Its feet are filthy!" shrieked Mum.
"It could have all kinds of strange diseases," warned Dad.
"Take it back to where you found it," they demanded,
both at the same time.
"It's lost," I said, but they had already started talking
about something else.

I hid the thing in our back shed and gave it something to eat, once I found out what it liked. It seemed a bit happier then, even though it was still lost.

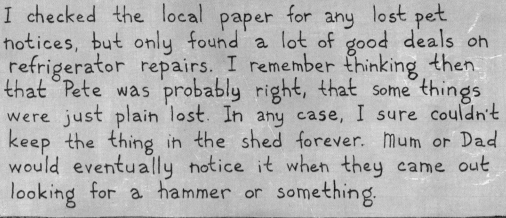

I checked the local paper for any lost pet notices, but only found a lot of good deals on refrigerator repairs. I remember thinking then that Pete was probably right, that some things were just plain lost. In any case, I sure couldn't keep the thing in the shed forever. Mum or Dad would eventually notice it when they came out looking for a hammer or something.

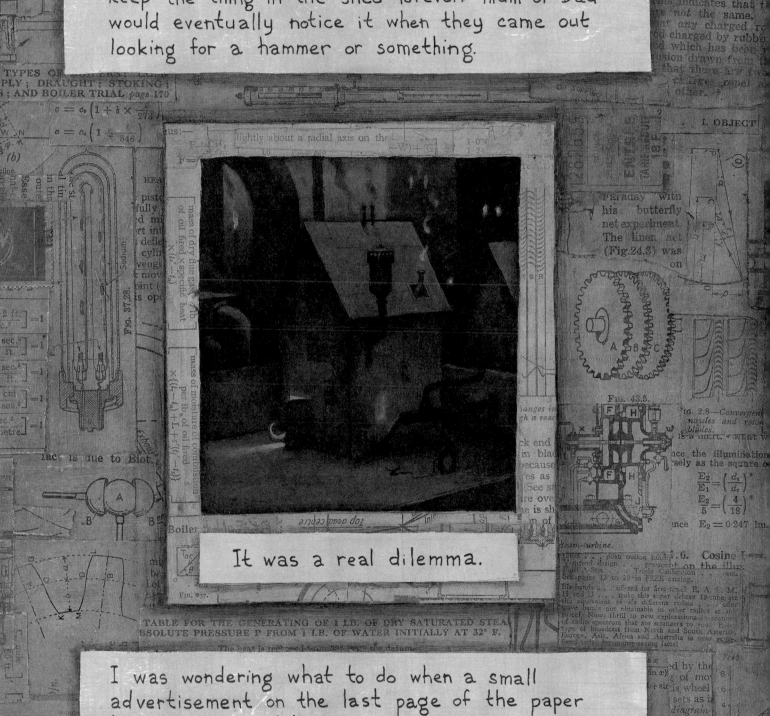

It was a real dilemma.

I was wondering what to do when a small advertisement on the last page of the paper happened to catch my eye.

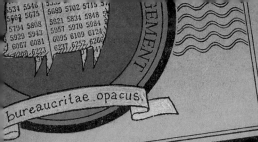

ARE **YOU** FINDING THAT
THE ORDER OF DAY-TO-DAY LIFE
IS UNEXPECTEDLY DISRUPTED BY

UNCLAIMED
PROPERTY?

OBJECTS
WITHOUT
NAMES?

TROUBLESOME
ARTIFACTS OF
UNKNOWN
ORIGIN?

FILING
CABINET
LEFTOVERS?

THINGS THAT
JUST DON'T
BELONG?

DON'T PANIC!

We've got a pigeon hole to stick it in.

THE FEDERAL DEPARTMENT OF ODDS & ENDS

sweepus underum carpetae.

Downtown,
6328th Street
Tall Grey Building #357b

The next morning we caught a tram into the city.

We arrived at a tall grey building with no windows. It was pretty dark in there, and it smelt like disinfectant. "I have a lost thing," I called to the receptionist at the front desk.
"Fill in these forms," she said.

The lost thing made a small, sad noise.

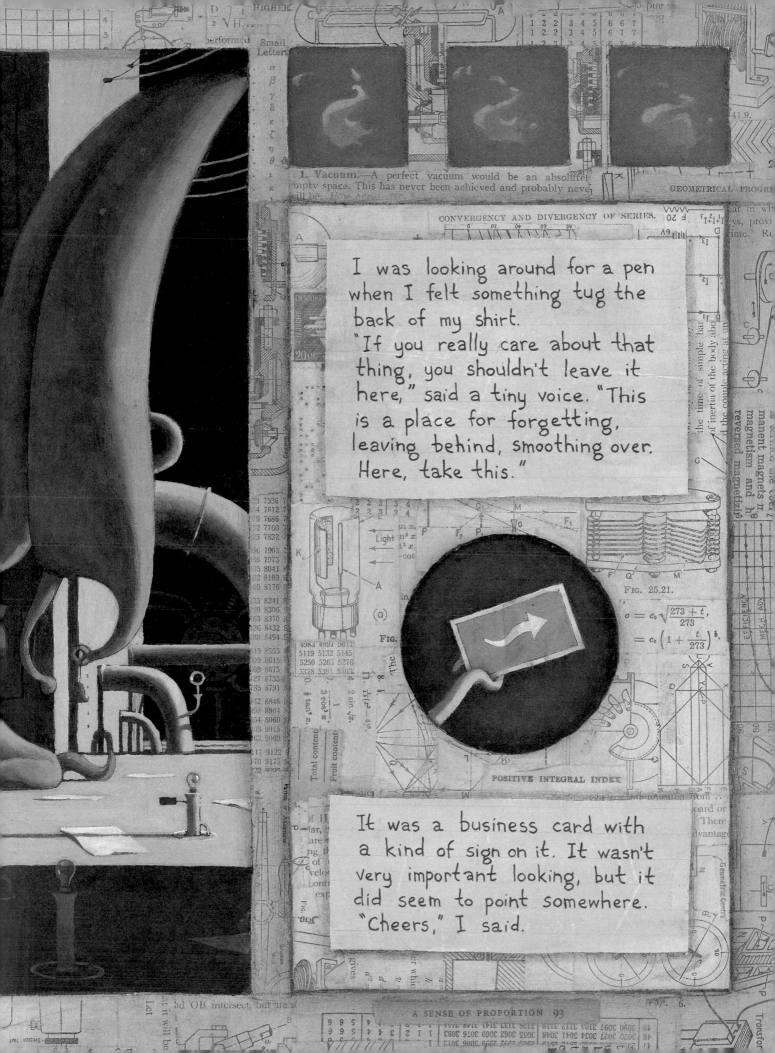

I was looking around for a pen when I felt something tug the back of my shirt.
"If you really care about that thing, you shouldn't leave it here," said a tiny voice. "This is a place for forgetting, leaving behind, smoothing over. Here, take this."

It was a business card with a kind of sign on it. It wasn't very important looking, but it did seem to point somewhere. "Cheers," I said.

At this point we left that tall grey building

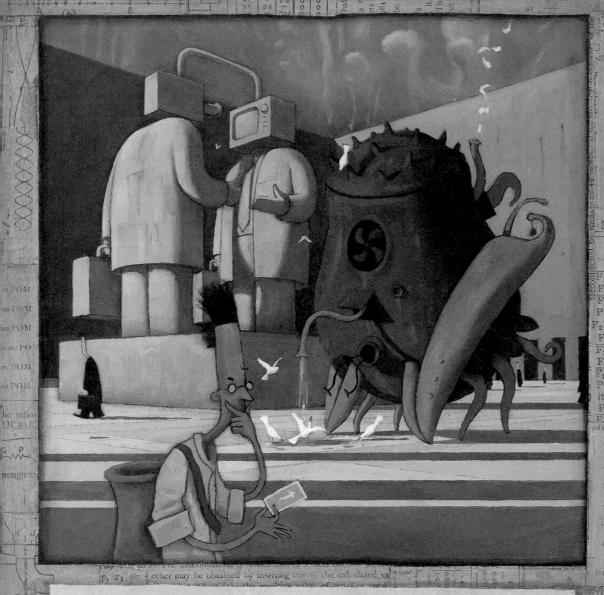

and hunted all over the place for this sign.

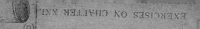

It wasn't an easy job,

TODAY IS THE
TOMORROW YOU
WERE PROMISED
YESTERDAY.

and I can't say I knew what it all meant.

Eventually we found what seemed to be the right place, in a dark little gap off some anonymous little street. The sort of place you'd never know existed unless you were actually looking for it.

I pressed a buzzer on the wall and this big door opened up.

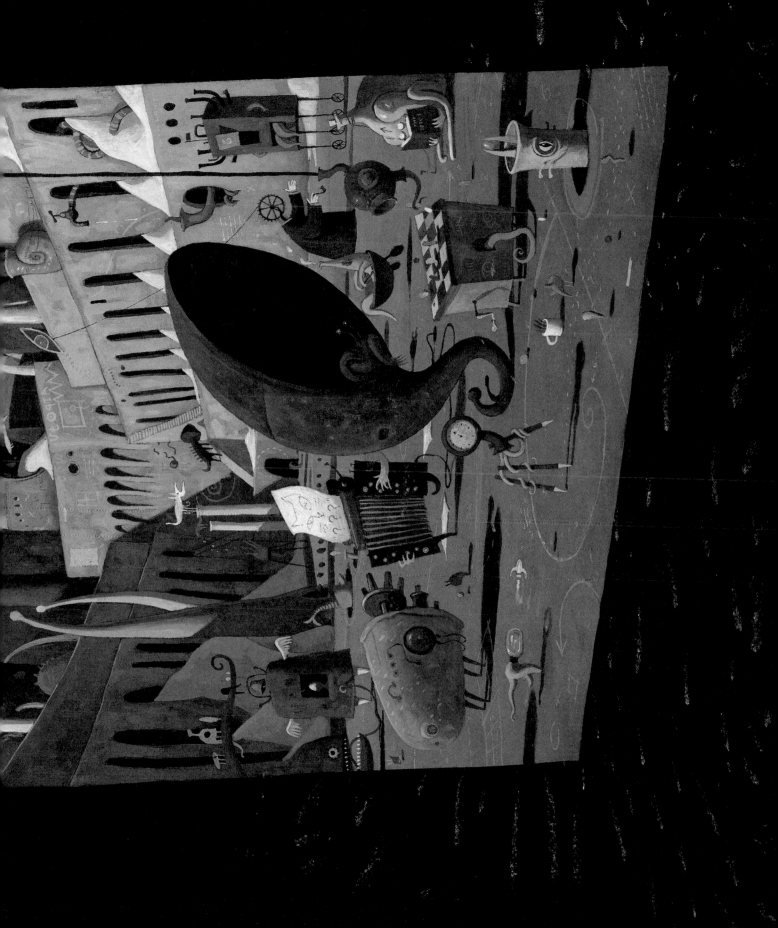

I didn't know what to think, but the lost thing made an approving sort of noise. It seemed as good a time as any to say good-bye to each other. So we did.

Then I went home to classify my bottle-top collection.

Well, that's it. That's the story.
Not especially profound, I know, but I
never said it was.
And don't ask me what the moral is.

I mean, I can't say that the thing
actually belonged in the place where it
ended up. In fact, none of the things
there really belonged. They all seemed
happy enough though, so maybe that
didn't matter. I don't know....

I still think about that lost thing from time to time. Especially when I see something out of the corner of my eye that doesn't quite fit.

You know, something with a weird, sad, lost sort of look.

I see that sort of thing less and less these days though.

Maybe there aren't many lost things around anymore.

Or maybe I've just stopped noticing them.

Too busy doing other stuff, I guess.

And APOLOGIES TO Edward Hopper & Jeffrey Smart, & John Brack

Paul & The Twins... A The Funkmeister A Gary Crew A BILL DAY, the freo lit centre folks, Jonathan, Keira, Robin, and for valued interest and comments from

with THANKS to Helen Chamberlin Chris D. a fellow connoisseur of heavy duty industrial plumbing

Editorial technician #264

node through the high resistance X Y and

the air in the clearance space should be made to expand reversibly and adiabatically, but little can be done towards ensuring this. The valves fitted to compressors are automatic on both suction

The Rabbits   Words by John Marsden

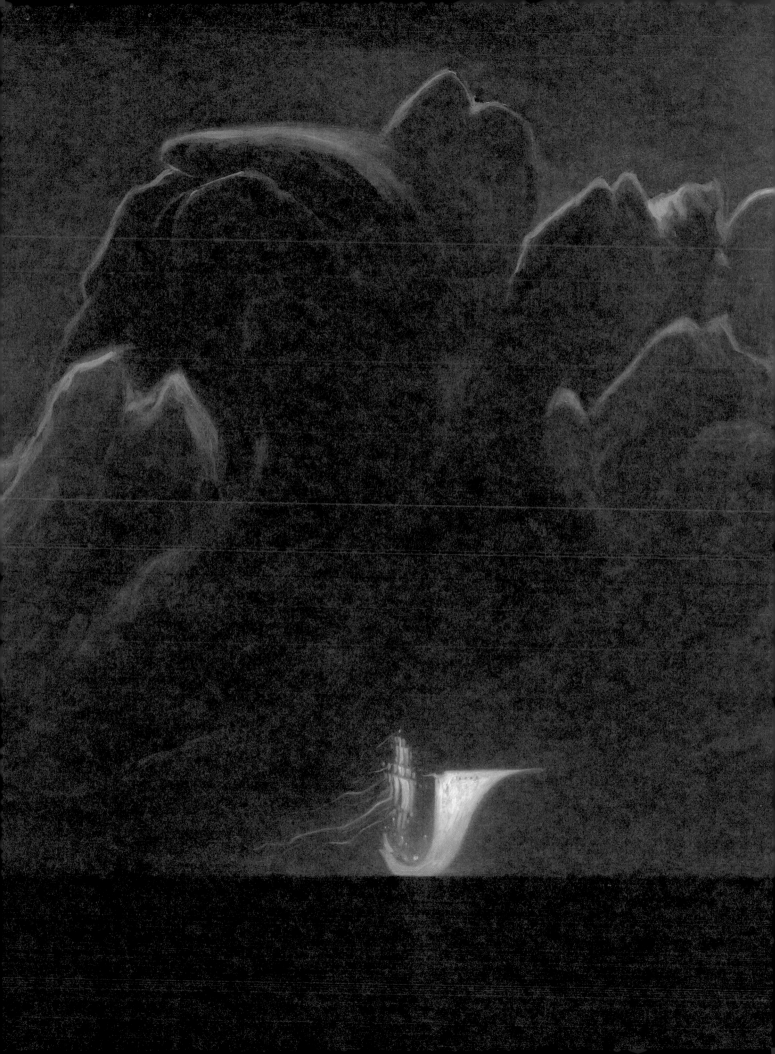

THE RABBITS CAME MANY GRANDPARENTS AGO.

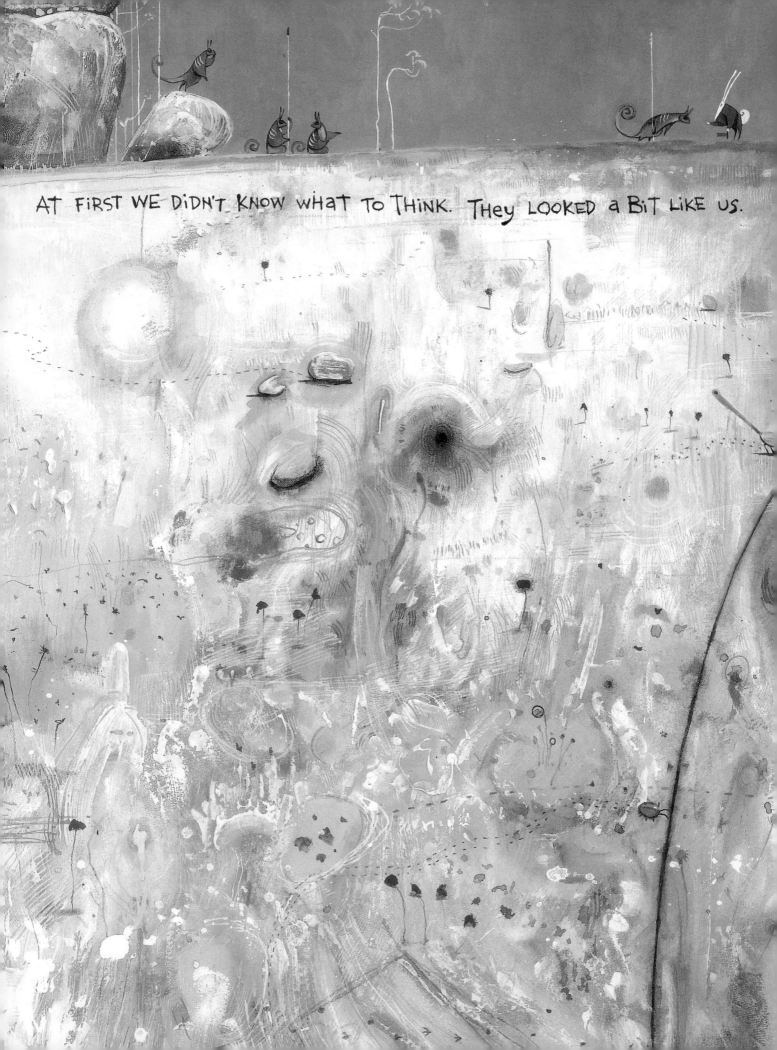

AT FIRST WE DIDN'T KNOW WHAT TO THINK. THEY LOOKED a BiT LIKE US.

THERE WEREN'T MANY OF THEM. SOME WERE FRIENDLY.

MORE RABBITS CAme...

THEY CAME BY WATER.

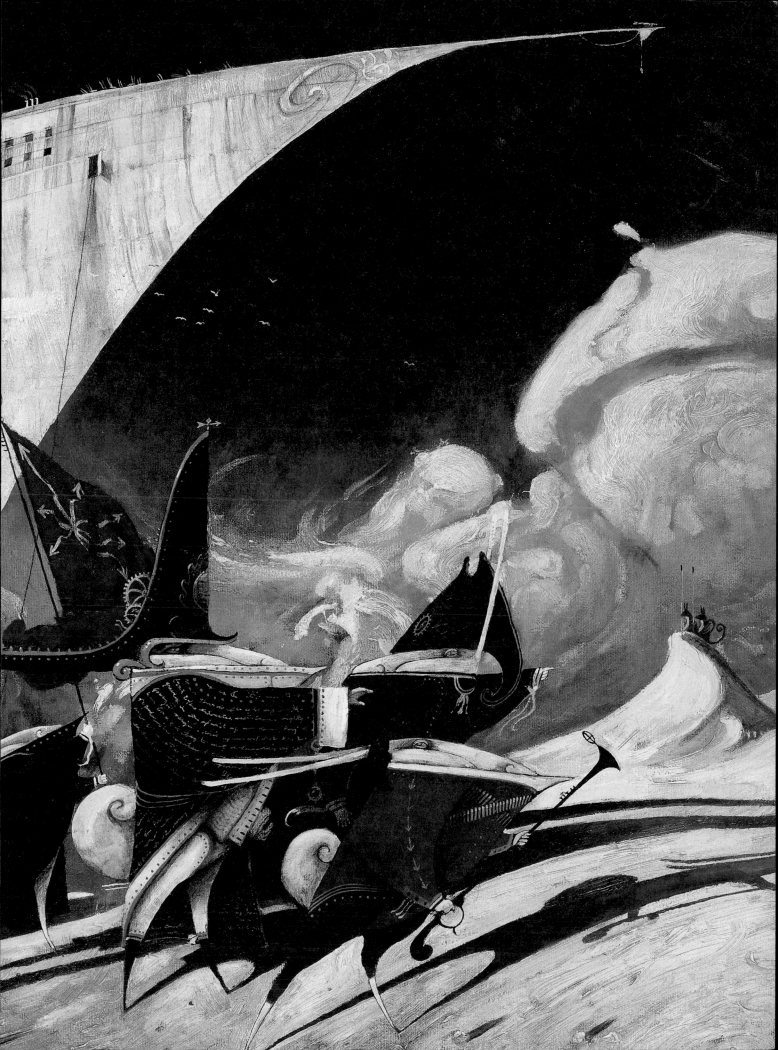

WE COULDN'T UNDERSTAND THE WAY THEY TALKED.

THEY BROUGHT NEW FOOD, AND THEY BROUGHT OTHER ANIMALS.

THE RABBITS SPREAD ACROSS THE COUNTRY.

NO MOUNTAIN COULD STOP THEM; NO DESERT, NO RIVER.

STILL MORE OF THEM CAME.

SOMETIMES WE HAD FIGHTS,

BUT THERE WERE TOO MANY RABBITS.

They ate our grass.

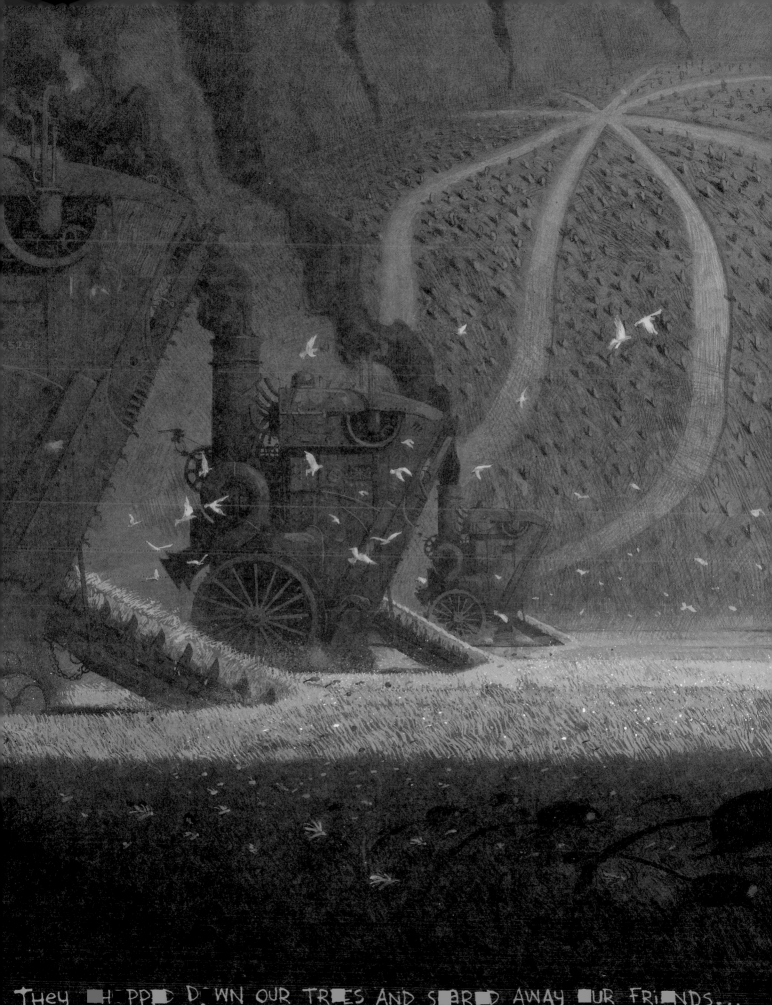

THEY CHIPPED DOWN OUR TREES AND SCARED AWAY OUR FRIENDS...

The Land is BARE and BROWN
and the WIND BLOWS EMPTY
across The Plains.

WHERE IS THE RICH, DARK EARTH,
BROWN AND MOIST?
WHERE IS THE SMELL OF RAIN
DRIPPING FROM THE GUM TREES?

WHERE ARE THE GREAT BILLABONGS,
THE RIVER-SWOLLEN LAKES,
ALIVE WITH LONG-LEGGED BIRDS?

WHO WILL SAVE US FROM THE RABBITS?